Disney

INFINITY

HERO CHALLENGE!

By Amy Weingartner
Illustrated by Fabio Laguna and James Gallego

Random House New York

 Published in the United States by Random House Children's Books, a division of Penguin Random House LLC, 1745 Broadway, New York, NY 10019, and in Canada by Random House of Canada, a division of Penguin Random House Ltd., Toronto. Random House and the colophon are registered trademarks of Penguin Random House LLC.

randomhousekids.com

For more information on Disney Infinity, please visit:
Disney.com/Infinity

ISBN 978-0-7364-3396-9 (trade)
ISBN 978-0-7364-8204-2 (lib. bdg.)

Printed in the United States of America

10 9 8 7 6 5 4 3 2 1

Chapter 1

High above the Toy Box, Anna and Hiro sat on the back of Baymax the robot as they cruised through the sky.

"Wow!" said Anna. "It's amazing up here!"

"Let's go around again, Baymax,"

said Hiro. Baymax dipped one wing and circled over the city buildings.

Hiro and Baymax were in the world of the Toy Box. A shooting star had transported them there. Anna had been transported by another shooting star. She had met Hiro and Baymax on a previous adventure in the Toy Box, so she'd agreed to go along for a ride on Baymax's back.

"What's going on down there?" asked Anna. Below them, an army of mechanical monsters were smashing buildings and flipping vehicles over.

Anna, Hiro, and Baymax watched the destruction from above.

“Those robots are not health-care companions,” Baymax replied.

Hiro laughed.

“How about if we land?” Anna pointed to where a girl was racing in a kart.

“Good idea,” said Hiro.

Vanellope von Schweetz drove her Candy Kart up and down a stretch of track. This wasn't her first visit to the Toy Box either.

"I like this town," she said to herself. "Something new happens every second!" She screeched to a halt to avoid bumping into a cowgirl in a wide-brimmed red hat. "Like meeting you, for instance! Howdy!" she said to the stranger. "You're a cowgirl, right?"

"You bet," said Jessie, "and that's some ride you got there! Can I try?"

"I'm Vanellope. Jump in!"

As they sped down the track, a huge red flying robot with two passengers

on its back landed in their path.

"Hey! I know you guys!" shouted Vanellope. "Anna! Hiro! And that big lug—good ol' Baymax."

"Howdy," said Jessie. "I'm Jessie. A star—"

"—brought you here," Vanellope interrupted. "Yeah, we know! The same thing happened to us, and it's happened before, too. That's how we know each other."

"What's going on in this city?" Hiro asked Vanellope. "Seems like metal monsters are destroying everything."

"Let's take a closer look," Hiro said.

Everyone leapt onto Baymax's back, and the red robot zoomed into the air. They watched the battle from high in the sky.

Dressed in red Super suits, the Incredibles defended the city from the attack. Mr. Incredible, Mrs. Incredible, and their children Dash and Violet had special powers.

"Take that!" said Mrs. Incredible. She

wrapped her elastic body around the robot's claw, disabling it.

Mr. Incredible smashed a robot with his amazing strength. "One more Omnidroid down," he said. He picked up another Omnidroid and threw it into a brick building. "Make that two more."

Nearby, a flame-haired villain was flying on a hoverboard, shouting commands to the Omnidroids. "Would you *please* destroy them?" he shouted.

"There are too many of those things for the heroes to fight!" said Jessie.

"The Omnidroids are bad news," said Hiro. "Baymax, run program TB0002 and see if you can detect how

to disable their big claws. Who wants to help?"

"I've got my shovel," said Anna. "I'm ready to try!"

"Me too," said Jessie.

"I do have a cherry bomb or two up my sleeve," said Vanellope. "On top of that, I'm feisty!"

"Okay," said Hiro. "Baymax, take us into battle!"

Chapter 2

Violet was holding back two giant Omnidroids with a force field when she heard a *whoosh* and saw a red robot land nearby.

In a flash, Dash sped over to the new arrivals. "Wow," he said. "It's *you* guys!" During another visit to the Toy Box, Dash had gone on an ice-race adventure with Anna, Hiro, Baymax, and Vanellope.

"Syndrome is attacking!" said Dash.

"What can we do?" said Jessie.

Just then, a short, round, one-eyed green fellow came up to the group. "I'm new around here. Hey, where's Randy? I was sure he came along when we saw the star. . . ."

"Who are you?" Vanellope asked.

"Pardon his lack of manners," said the lizardlike creature who seemed to appear out of nowhere. "I'm Randy. That's Mike. We're monsters."

"Yeah, but the only scary things here are those guys!" Mike pointed at the Omnidroids.

Just then, Mrs. Incredible called, "Violet, Dash! We need you."

"Mom, look—new friends!" said Dash. "They want to help us battle Syndrome!"

Mrs. Incredible looked the group over. Besides Violet and Dash, there was a young red-haired woman with a shovel, a boy in a high-tech hero suit, a big robot, a cowgirl, a small girl eating a lollipop, a short green fellow with one eye, and a lizard.

"You all do not exactly look ready to

fight," she said. "Do you have any special abilities?"

"Sure we do," said Hiro. "I can control tiny robots called microbots."

He turned to the group. "You, uh, *do* have abilities, right, guys?"

"Glitching!" said Vanellope proudly. "It might not sound helpful, but I'm great at it!"

Anna held up her grappling hook in one hand and her shovel in the other. "I can dig and I can climb!"

Mike put his arms up and made a frightening face. "I can scare," said Mike.

"Also scare," said Randy. Then he blended into the surroundings, turning invisible. "And I can disappear like this. It's kind of a stealth mode."

Hiro looked at Jessie.

"Yo-de-lay-hee-hoooo!" she shouted. The sound echoed off the buildings. "And I've been known to rustle a varmint or two."

"Yodeling. Now, *that's* different," Mike said to himself.

"Okay, great," said Hiro. "Mike and Jessie, you'll help Dash. Vanellope and Randy, you'll help Violet. Anna and I will help Mrs. Incredible."

"What exactly do we do?" said Mike.

"Just follow us," said Hiro. "No time to explain!"

In a town square, Mr. Incredible was tossing Omnidroids against a building. Only a few of them were left.

Everyone jumped off Baymax.

"Let's go," said Dash. "The goal is just to crush these Omnidroids . . ."

". . . without letting them crush you!" finished Violet.

"What about that awful guy on the hoverboard?" said Anna.

"That's Syndrome. If you couldn't guess, he's the bad guy!" said Dash.

Dash, Mike, and Jessie ran toward an Omnidroid that was swinging its arms and smashing windows.

"Arrgh!" said Mike, making a scary face. The Omnidroid took a swing at Mike and he tumbled across the park.

"Stop that!" Jessie yelled at the metal monster. She took a deep breath. *"Yo-de-lay-hee-hoooo!"*

"Watch out behind you!" called Dash. He pushed Jessie out of the path of an oncoming Omnidroid.

Dash used super-speedy punches

to throw it off-balance. "Another one down!" he cheered enthusiastically.

Violet created a force field to hold off the last of the Omnidroids, while Vanellope used her glitching power to keep out of its reach.

"Where's Randy?" said Violet.

Randy had become invisible and bravely climbed to the top of the Omnidroid. He managed to pull out a few wires before it grabbed him and tossed him into a Dumpster.

"Over here," said Randy, becoming visible again.

"Nice work," said Violet.

While they battled the last of the

Omnidroids, Syndrome hovered overhead. "Destroy them!" he commanded. But Mrs. Incredible threw a stretch punch and blocked a blow from its long metal claw.

Thwack! Anna hit the metal arm with her shovel, cracking it. As the Omnidroid turned its electric eye on her, Anna tossed her grappling hook against a building and swung up. "Hiro!" she called when the robot changed targets and moved toward him. "Behind you!"

Hiro ducked away from the Omnidroid's claw just in time. He touched the transmitter on his helmet to form a wall of microbots to block the next attack.

Mr. Incredible threw a punch that smashed the Omnidroid. "And that takes care of that," he said.

"For now," added Mrs. Incredible. "Thanks for your help, everyone."

"We know they'll be back," said Dash.

"We need to prepare for next time," said Violet.

"I have an idea," said Mrs. Incredible. "Anyone interested in a little challenge? Who wants to learn how to be a hero?"

Chapter 3

"What, you mean like taking lessons?" said Jessie.

"I mean training—hero training."

"What will you teach us?" asked Anna.

"Well," said Mrs. Incredible, "the basics, like flying, jumping . . ."

“Racing cars,” said Dash.

“Search-and-rescue,” Violet added.

“Hey, look,” said Hiro. “Who is that guy smashing things?”

Across the city park, Wreck-It Ralph was tossing mailboxes.

“He’s not smashing—he’s wrecking!” said Vanellope. “That’s Ralph!”

“Oh, hey,” Ralph said, and dropped a car he had just lifted.

"That's impressive," Anna said.

"Wrecking? It comes easy for me," said Ralph.

"I see," said Mrs. Incredible. "We're doing hero training here. Maybe you could use your wrecking for good. Since you like to break things, you should team up with Mr. Incredible."

Ralph and Mr. Incredible fist-bumped and said in unison, "Wreck and roll."

"Teaming up, I see," said a voice from above. "An interesting move."

The heroes and trainees looked up to see Syndrome on his hover-board. He let out an evil cackle:

"*Mwwa-hahaha-hahaha!*"

"Get ready!" Mr. Incredible said to everyone.

"See, that's my concern," said Mike. "When I'm told to 'get ready,' I have no idea what to do."

"You're right about having *no ideas,*" said Randy.

"Now, listen," said Syndrome. "I've always been a villain. I would really like to try to be a hero for once."

"You can't trust him," said Violet.

"Let's hear him out," said Mrs. Incredible. She looked up at Syndrome. "If we train you in how to be a hero, what will you do for us?"

"*I* will help you understand the mind of the villain," he replied.

He zoomed toward the ground and jumped off his hoverboard.

"We'll give it a try," Mr. Incredible said. "Mrs. Incredible and I will keep an eye on you."

"*Mwah-ha-ha-ha* . . . er . . . um . . . I mean, marvelous!" Syndrome said, clearing his throat.

"We'll start with flying and racing vehicles," Mrs. Incredible anounced. "Let's split up into two groups and meet back here to review the lessons."

"Eww, that word again . . . *lessons,*" Vanellope grumbled.

Mr. and Mrs. Incredible and Violet led Randy, Ralph, Mike, and Syndrome to the track. Along the way, they discovered a monster truck, a red race car, a tow truck, and other vehicles.

The strongest team members, Ralph and Mr. Incredible, helped create the obstacle course with trucks and boulders.

They began the first lesson. "Racing is not just a matter of speed," said Violet. "It's about paying attention and avoiding obstacles."

"Sometimes you must go around an obstacle, and other times jump over it," said Mrs. Incredible.

They fired up their engines. Mike went first in the Candy Kart. He hit the gas and immediately shot backward, almost crashing into his team.

"Watch it!" Syndrome growled.

"You're supposed to go *that way,*" said Randy, pointing down the track.

"Heroes don't bully," said Mrs. Incredible.

His next try was better. Mike zoomed down the track until he saw that two trucks blocked his path, leaving him only a narrow space.

With no time to decide, Mike headed for the space between the trucks and got stuck. Violet ran over to him.

"I was maybe supposed to go *around* them?" Mike asked.

"Next time try that," said Violet.

Next up was Randy in a monster truck with huge wheels. When he reached the two trucks, he sped up.

"Team, listen up," said Mrs. Incredible. "He should be *slowing down* when approaching an obstacle."

Randy tried to jump over the trucks. He landed on top of the first truck. His monster truck teetered on it like a seesaw.

"I'll get you down," said Mrs. Incredible, stretching herself to help him off the truck. "Jumping obstacles is not a beginner move."

"Let me try," said Ralph in his red race car. When he got to the truck obstacles, he slowed down. He stopped and got out of the car, then smashed both trucks and tossed them aside.

Mrs. Incredible blew a whistle while Mr. Incredible reset the course. "Okay, trainees," she said, "there is one thing you must remember: *never stop and get out of your vehicle* during a race!"

Chapter 4

"My turn!" said Syndrome, revving the engine. He took his big-wheeled coach down the track and maneuvered around the trucks. Then he turned a corner and saw three large boulders in his way. He screeched to a stop.

"This is impossible!" he shouted. "How can I be expected to get around these ridiculous rocks?" Using his zero-point energy gauntlets, Syndrome moved the boulders.

Mrs. Incredible sighed. "Note, class, that one does not always have zero-point energy to blast obstacles."

"Syndrome, that was not hero behavior," said Mr. Incredible. "Here's how it's done."

Mr. Incredible got into a green race car and sped up. He maneuvered around the trucks and headed toward the boulders. He steered the car up the smooth rock surface, over the top, and down the other side.

“Speed and control are the keys to racing,” said Mrs. Incredible while everyone watched. “Panic and tantrums are *not* hero options.”

“How about the option to forget this training?” Syndrome whispered to Randy. “Go have some fun?”

“I heard that,” Mike said to Randy, eyeing him suspiciously.

At the top of a skyscraper near a waterfront, away from the racing lessons, Dash, Hiro, and Baymax were teaching Vanellope, Anna, and Jessie to fly.

"Speed and flying are essential tools for any hero. You can use them to survey the enemy, find tools and vehicles, go on rescue missions, and even escape!" said Dash.

"Plus," said Hiro, "flying is cool!"

"Baymax is going to demonstrate some key hero flying moves, and then everyone can try," said Hiro.

Baymax deployed his wings and jumped off the edge of the building. He went into a nosedive and then soared upward. They watched as he dipped his right wing to go right, and his left wing to go left.

Baymax returned to the group. "I have completed my mission. Is everyone satisfied with the flying demonstration?"

"That was great, Baymax," said Jessie. "But how are we going to fly without wings?"

Hiro and Dash held out some glide packs. "With these," Dash said.

"Where did you get those?" said Jessie.

"That's what's amazing about this place," said Hiro. "We smashed open a box over there and found them."

"My dad uses glide packs all the time," said Dash. "They're pretty fun, but you have to learn to control them."

Dash put a black-and-red glide pack on his back. He raced over to a water tower on top of the building. Then he power-jumped his way up the side to give himself a little more height.

"Here goes!" Dash called out, leaping off the water tower. Yellow wings shot out of the glide pack, and he took off into the sky!

"Yee-*hah*!" said Jessie.

Dash circled above the group while he called out instructions. "Catch the wind under your wings to go up. Dive headfirst to go toward the ground." He demonstrated a few short turns over their heads. Then he landed.

Jessie, Anna, and Vanellope took turns learning to use the glide packs. None of them had learned power-jumping yet—so first, Baymax gave Anna a lift to the top of the water tower.

"I will be ready to catch you if necessary," Baymax said.

Anna nodded and jumped off with a big grin on her face. Her wings came out right away and she took flight. "Wow!" she said. "This is amazing!"

"You're a natural," said Hiro.

"I'm next!" said Vanellope.

Baymax took her up. She stood on the edge of the water tower and looked down. Suddenly, she was dizzy. The group on the ground started to spin. "I feel sick," she said. "I think I'm afraid of heights."

"Fear is a natural response," said Baymax.

"Close your eyes," said Jessie. "Don't look down for the first few seconds."

"Let's try it again," said Dash. "I'll go with you." He grabbed Vanellope's hand, and she shut her eyes. "One . . . two . . . three . . ." And off they jumped.

Vanellope's wings came out and she

was airborne. "Whoopee!" she cried.

"Keep yourself level," said Dash. "Now nose down, bring your feet around, that's it! And now land!"

"I think I'm going to love flying," said Vanellope. "Bring on the bad guys!"

Jessie went next. She took a big breath. "Here I go!" she called as she closed her eyes and jumped.

"That's right, Jessie!" Dash said, encouraging her. "Keep it moving, head down, you got it. Perfect landing!"

Chapter 5

The new flyers perfected their moves while gliding over to the rest of the team at the track.

"Welcome, flyers," said Mrs. Incredible. "Racers, switch and go with Dash, Baymax, and Hiro."

"I'll just kick back during this lesson," said Vanellope.

"Heroes always have to be prepared and they don't eat too many sweets," said Mr. Incredible. "Let's go, Von Schweetz!"

Anna and Jessie got into different vehicles. Mr. and Mrs. Incredible led them through the same series of racing lessons the others had just taken.

Meanwhile, the new flyers went up to the water tower on Baymax's back. Once both teams had gone through the racing and flying training, they gathered together as one big group.

"Now we're going to use the skills

you just learned for a mission," said Mr. Incredible. "The team that finds the most tools and coins in one hour wins."

"Being a hero is a team effort," said Hiro.

"Whose team am I on?" said Mike.

"You'll find out soon," said Mrs. Incredible. "You're a team captain! Anna is the other captain."

"I pick Ralph," said Mike. "I like having a big guy around."

"I pick Syndrome," said Anna.

"Thank you," Syndrome said with a curt nod. "At least someone recognizes talent."

Next, Ralph convinced Mike that

Randy's ability to blend in with his surroundings could really help the team.

"Vanellope for us," said Anna.

"Jessie's ours!" said Mike.

Team Mike was made up of Randy, Ralph, and Jessie. On Team Anna were Syndrome and Vanellope—and Violet joined them to make the teams even. The heroes would guide and watch both groups.

The teams went into the area of the Toy Box where tall buildings surrounded a city park. Around the park and in the buildings were hidden coins, chests, vaults, and tools.

"Take an elevator up to the top of each building," said Mr. Incredible. "On the roofs you will find coins and treasure. Use your glide packs to fly down and deliver them."

"Use the vehicles to search the streets around the park," said Mrs. Incredible.

"Teamwork is essential," Hiro said. "We'll be watching to make sure each group is working together."

Team Mike rode up an elevator in a building with big windows.

Team Anna was headed for the building next door when Syndrome stopped them.

"Let's take my hoverboard," he said. "We can get around faster!"

"Is it okay to use a shortcut?" said Vanellope, eyeing Syndrome.

Syndrome gave her and Anna a look that said there was always more than one way to do something.

"Let's try it," Anna said.

Violet frowned, but didn't say anything. She knew that heroes sometimes had to find their own way.

As soon as they reached the roof, Vanellope spotted a vault and tried to open it. No luck. "You try it, Syndrome!" she said. The redheaded would-be hero was able to smash it with a blast of zero-point energy.

"Score!" Vanellope and Syndrome said triumphantly in unison.

Anna took the coins that popped out. She opened her glide pack and jumped off the building, making a smooth landing next to the delivery spot in the park.

Vanellope launched off the top of the building and landed on a ledge. Hopping along, she found glowing, sparkly balls with coins inside.

Syndrome easily mastered power-jumping up walls and drainpipes, but he grumbled when he couldn't find any more treasure.

"I think you've all got it . . . mostly," Violet told the team.

Team Mike struggled to work together.

"Look at Syndrome," said Randy from another rooftop. "He's up to no good."

"Why do you care?" said Mike.

"I just don't think it's fair," said Randy, "how *Syndrome* gets to be a hero when he's really a *villain*."

"We're going to help good citizens everywhere be safe from the terrible things with claws!" said Mike.

"But Syndrome *created* the things

with claws!" said Randy. "Why does he get to be a hero?"

"We have to give him a chance, Randy," said Mike.

"It's what heroes do," Jeese added. "And you want to be a hero, right?"

Randy nodded. Ralph patted him on the back. He knew it was difficult to be a good guy sometimes.

When the hour was up, Mrs. Incredible blew her whistle. Everyone gathered in the park to take score. Team Anna did better than Team Mike at unlocking vaults and smashing the glowing balls. Team Anna made a large pile of coins, gadgets, and tools they had uncovered, including paintball and slime blasters.

"I can barely buy a sandwich with this money," said Mike, looking at their tiny pile of coins.

"You've got another chance coming," said Mrs. Incredible. "The heroes and villains challenge is next."

She and Mr. Incredible divided up

the the two teams. Mike, Randy, Ralph, Syndrome, and Violet would now be Team Villain. They would play against Anna, Jessie, and Vanellope, who would be Team Hero.

"And I'll join the heroes just to make things more interesting for my sister," Dash said.

"Bring it on, bro," Violet replied.

The battle was on!

Chapter 6

In the park, Hiro gave everyone instructions.

"Villains, you must devise a scheme to outwit the heroes, grab one of their team members, and wreak at least *some* havoc on the city."

"That will be a piece of cake," said Syndrome.

"Drats. That's just an expression, isn't it?" said Vanellope.

Mr. Incredible continued with the instructions. "Heroes, you must avoid losing a team member to the other side—or, if one of you is taken, then together you must go on a rescue mission."

"I stand ready to engage my health-care matrix," said Baymax.

"Don't worry, Baymax," Hiro said with a laugh. "Everyone will come through this villain challenge just fine."

Baymax flew the two teams to

different areas near the edge of the water.

"Ready?" said Hiro. "Go!"

Right away, Team Hero found an abandoned fort that would serve as the perfect headquarters. Dash took up position in the turret overlooking the fort.

On another part of the island, Team Villain was arguing about who they should capture.

"Jessie knows how to untie ropes, so she's out," said Mike. "And that Dash kid is way too fast."

"Anna has that shovel with her—she can dig her way out of anything!" said

Wreck-It Ralph with admiration.

"What about Vanellope?" said Randy.

"Good idea," said Syndrome. "I knew you'd be a good villain."

"But we're not really going to *really* capture her, right?" Mike asked.

"It's part of the challenge!" said Randy, exasperated.

"I just don't think it's polite," Mike replied.

"But the point is we are villains!" said Randy.

"Stop arguing," said Violet. "We're *playing* villains, remember? It's just part of our mission. And they have to attempt a rescue as part of *their* mission to be heroes."

Syndrome looked at Violet. "I never thought the day would come when I agreed with an Incredible," he said.

"Okay, okay," said Mike. "Let's go for Vanellope."

The villain fired up his hoverboard. "I'm going to show you how it's done!" he said, taking off into the air.

Syndrome cruised over to the fort, where Dash stood at the top of the tower. Anna and Jessie were stationed at the windows. Vanellope was on the fort's wall.

The flying villain swooped in and

began an attack with plasma blasters and exploding cherry bombs.

"Fire!" said Vanellope, shooting a paintball blaster.

Syndrome dodged her blast. He circled the trees and the fort, then flew out of sight.

"We scared him off!" said Anna.

"I doubt it," said Dash. "Syndrome doesn't scare that easily."

Suddenly, the team heard a cry from the tree and saw Syndrome flying away with Vanellope.

"He's got Vanellope!" shouted Anna. "Heroes, engage the rescue plan!"

"You got it!" said Jessie.

"I can't believe you got me!" Vanellope grumbled at Syndrome. "You're like a sour candy with sand on it. Blech!"

On the hoverboard, Syndrome was holding on to her so she couldn't jump off and fly with her glide pack.

"I'll take that as a compliment, but be quiet. I have to concentrate," he ordered her.

"In that case," she said, and yelled, "Hey! Everyone! Syndrome got me!" Her shouts echoed above the trees and over the little island.

"Guys! I hear Vanellope!" said Ralph.

Team Villain raced out into the open and saw Syndrome flying toward them. He hovered over the group.

"Good work, Syndrome," Violet said.

"It was easy," he replied, looking down at Violet. "The truth is . . . I like being bad. And I don't think I need Team Villain anymore. *Mwah-ha-ha-ha-ha*."

"No! Wait!" called Ralph. He felt helpless as he watched Syndrome fly away with his short, sweet pal. "We have to help her!"

"No, we're villains. This is just a training mission!" Randy replied.

"I'm not so sure," said Ralph.

"I don't trust Syndrome," Mike replied. "We have to go after them."

"I think our mission just changed," Violet said. "Who wants to be a hero?"

Everyone cheered.

"Good," Violet said. "Then let's go."

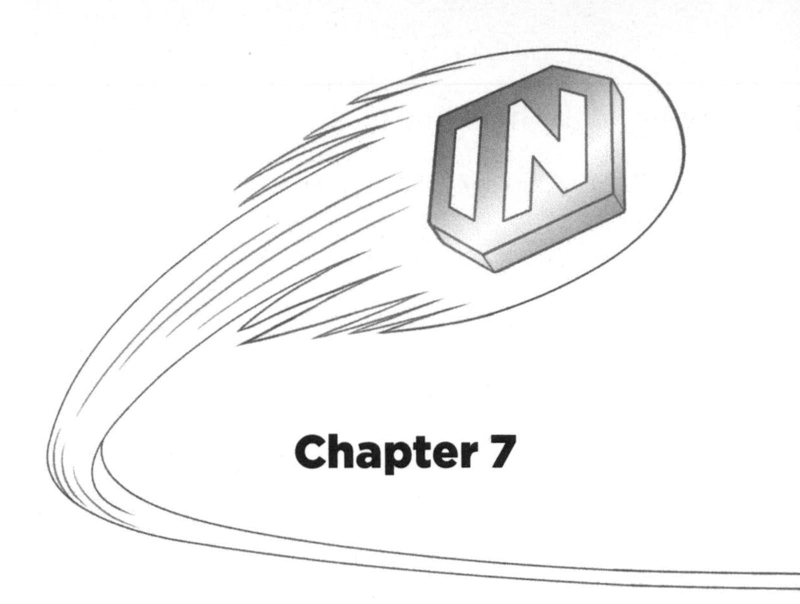

Chapter 7

At the fort, Team Hero gathered their weapons and tools to help Vanellope. They had a flamingo croquet mallet, a paintball blaster, green plasma blasters, a slime blaster, and some cherry bombs.

"I have an idea where he might have taken her," said Dash.

At the edge of the island were some vehicles, which they boarded to race over the bridges into the city. Dash led the group to the bottom of a tall, dark building.

"This looks like one of Syndrome's lairs," he said. "I noticed it when we arrived in the Toy Box."

"And there's a big *S* painted on the side," Jessie said.

"That too," Dash replied.

Just then, Violet, Ralph, Randy, and Mike arrived.

"Hey! Have you seen Vanellope?"

Ralph asked. "Syndrome's gone bad."

"You mean Syndrome isn't just pretending?" Jessie asked.

"I hate to say it, but I told you so," Randy said to Mike.

"If we work together, we can defeat him and find her," Mike said.

"Find who?" said a voice behind them. "I love a mystery!"

Everyone turned around. Vanellope was relaxing on a hoverboard, licking a lollipop.

"Vanellope! You're okay!" Ralph cried with joy.

"Okay as candy. Syndrome flew me over here to his lair. He was

being all stinky and villainy, but then I remembered: I can glitch. Duh. It's like I have a superpower," Vanellope explained, turning herself fuzzy as she glitched off the hoverboard and onto the ground. "So I glitched a little, and just like that, I was free."

"Syndrome is not going to like this," said Randy.

"I appreciate being the subject of everyone's conversation," said

Syndrome. He hovered over them, his rocket boots flaring. "But maybe you should worry about yourselves!"

Suddenly, the huge claw of an Omnidroid grabbed Mike.

"Whoa!" he said.

"How's *that* for a lesson in being a villain?" Syndrome let out a big laugh. "Come and get me . . . *heroes.*"

The united teams called in Mr. and Mrs. Incredible, Baymax, and Hiro. This time, the hero challenge was real.

"Attack!" Syndrome called as he

flew back and forth overhead. A terrible noise filled the air, and dozens of Omnidroids were dropped from a flying vehicle.

"Oh, I don't like this," said Mr. Incredible.

"I'd love to stay and watch, but I've got places to be," Syndrome said. "While you're busy here, I'm going to find that shooting star back home, and Metroville will be all mine."

Syndrome turned and fired his rocket boots. He shot into the sky, taking Mike with him.

"We've got to go after him!" Hiro shouted.

"It's time for some leadership, heroes," Anna said. "Let's prove we can figure this out."

"Mrs. Incredible, you and the big boys—Mr. Incredible, Baymax, and Ralph—keep these Omnidroids busy," Randy said, suddenly feeling in charge.

"Syndrome flew that way," said Vanellope, pointing toward the bay in the distance.

"Violet and I can turn invisible," Randy added, starting to see a plan. "We can search for him ahead of you."

"And the rest of us can take the vehicles," said Jessie. "If we're fast, we can catch that varmint."

They jumped onto their vehicles and revved the engines, heading toward the bay. When they got to the edge of the water, Dash noticed a pirate ship that hadn't been there before.

Dash shouted, "Liftoff!" Everyone popped the wings on their glide packs. One by one, the heroes landed quietly on the deck of the ship.

Randy blended into the wooden deck. He quietly crawled over to Syndrome, who was standing at the captain's wheel. Mike was tied up!

Syndrome turned to Randy. "Did you think it would be that easy?" he said, directing the ship into open water.

Chapter 8

"Not so fast," said Jessie. She had picked up the rope and formed a lasso. She threw it around Syndrome and tied him to the mast.

"You will be terribly sorry, cowgirl!" Syndrome snarled.

"Yo-de-lay-hee-hoooo!" Jessie sang.

Syndrome was instantly stunned!

"Wow, that yodel is impressive," Mike said as the cowgirl untied him.

"Let's go before Syndrome gets his strength back!" said Anna, standing over him with her shovel.

They headed for shore, where the Incredibles, Baymax, Hiro, and Ralph had just finished crushing the Omnidroids.

"Is everyone satisfied with their care?" asked Baymax.

The heroes laughed. "Everyone except Syndrome," said Jessie.

They looked down. Syndrome

squirmed on the ground, trying to untie himself.

"Let him *try* to get out of that knot," said Jessie. "Whoever said a cowgirl couldn't survive in the big city?"

Now that the Toy Box was safe again, Mrs. Incredible complimented everyone on their bravery.

"Well done!" she said. "You all made very good heroes."

"And now we need to finish the job," said Mr. Incredible. "Let's release Syndrome."

"What?" said Mike.

"Release him?" said Ralph. "But he captured Mike—and Vanellope!"

"That's right," said Mr. Incredible. "And that's what super villains do. Bad things."

"We, however, are *not* super villains," said Mrs. Incredible.

"Sorry, guys," said Dash. "That's what it's like to be a hero. You always have to be good!"

Jessie untied the knot while the others stood guard.

"You were a very good villain, as always," said Mrs. Incredible.

"Well, you can't be heroes without a

villain," Syndrome said. "And I enjoyed being a good guy . . . for just a little while."

"It's so true," Ralph said, slapping Syndrome on the back.

Syndrome grimaced and rubbed his shoulder. He looked up and saw a shooting star.

"It's time for this villain to go!" Syndrome said. He let out a big evil laugh. "Next time we meet, I will claim victory!" A glittery sparkle of lights covered him. And with a sudden *whoosh*, he was gone.

"It looks like our stars are here, too," said Violet. "That was so much fun. You

guys made great heroes."

"Yes," said Dash. "Was it harder than you thought it would be?"

"Much harder," said Anna. "Do you ever get to rest?"

"No," said Mr. Incredible. "There are no vacations when it comes to fighting evil." He looked around at the team of new heroes. "Goodbye, heroes. Good luck!"

More stars appeared in the dark blue sky.

"That's us," said Hiro. "Baymax and I are going home."

"We'll miss you guys," said Mike.

"Yeah, but— Hey, look! It's our star," said Randy, taking Mike by the arm.

"Just hang on a minute," said Mike, pushing him away. "I'm saying goodbye! You know, the real challenge is putting up with *you.*"

Anna laughed. "Always fighting, you two. My star is next. Goodbye, everyone. Let's get together for another great adventure soon!"

"*Yee-haw!*" said Jessie. "You got it!" More shooting stars passed overhead.

Whoosh. Whoosh. Whoosh.

And then everyone was gone. The Toy Box was quiet . . . but for how long?

THE END?